WHEN IT'S SIX O'CLOCK IN SAN FRANCISCO

A TRIP THROUGH TIME ZONES

by Cynthia Jaynes Omololu

Illustrated by Randy DuBurke

Clarion Books

Houghton Mifflin Harcourt

Boston • New York

2009

It's six o'clock in San Francisco. "Time to get up," Mom calls from downstairs. Jared shivers, feeling the cold wood floor against his bare feet. Lifting a corner of the curtain, he peeks out the window at the fingers of fog reaching over the hills. He smells bacon cooking, and his stomach starts to rumble. Jumping the last two steps, he heads toward the kitchen calling, "Is the cocoa ready yet?"

SAN FRANCISCO

* THE SCENES IN THIS BOOK TAKE PLACE ON FEBRUARY 19th AND 20th.

When it's six o'clock in San Francisco, it's nine o'clock in Montréal. Geneviève squints up at the tall buildings as she and Papa emerge from the Metro. A faint chiming sounds in the distance. "Was that the bell?" she asks. "We must hurry!" Grabbing Papa's hand, she starts to run toward the school gates.

SAN FRANCISCO   MONTRÉAL

4

"Wait, Geneviève," Papa calls, "the sidewalk is very ic—"
But the rest is lost as they slip and slide on a wide patch
of ice. *Bang!* Down goes Papa. *Thump!* Geneviève lands
next to him.

"Are you okay?" Geneviève asks with a worried look.
Papa sits up, laughing, as they sprawl on the sidewalk.
"Très bien," he says, and gives Geneviève a kiss on both cheeks.

SAN FRANCISCO   MONTRÉAL

When he is back on his feet, he reaches down to help her up. "But now, let's hurry a little more slowly."

When it's six o'clock in San Francisco, it's eleven o'clock in Santiago. Elena's tongue sticks in the corner of her mouth as she rubs at the math problem with her eraser. Blowing the pink shreds of rubber off her desk, she notices a crumpled piece of paper at her feet.

"Psst," hisses Maria, two rows over. Elena turns to look.

"Read it." Maria's lips move, but there is no sound in the quiet classroom. Bending to retrieve the note, Elena hears a chair scrape at the front of the room.

SAN FRANCISCO   MONTRÉAL   SANTIAGO

"Elena," Maestra Portilla's voice booms. "Is there something you would like to share with the class?"

LONDON - 2:00 P.M.

When it's six o'clock in San Francisco, it's two o'clock in London. Oliver's knees are red with cold, but he's running so hard he doesn't feel it. His feet pound the grass, the ball spinning with each kick toward the goal that's looming straight ahead. But as soon as he's close enough to shoot, a tangle of legs blocks his path.

SAN FRANCISCO   MONTRÉAL   SANTIAGO   LONDON

"Through!" his teammate calls from across the field. Oliver kicks the ball in his direction. Seconds later, it's whizzing into the net.

SAN FRANCISCO   MONTRÉAL   SANTIAGO   LONDON

"Goal!" his teammates cry, high-fives all around. The bell echoes across the yard: Game over. The boys pick up their gear and head slowly back to class.

CAPE TOWN - 4:00 P.M.

When it's six o'clock in San Francisco, it's four o'clock in Cape Town. The rain falls hard and fast, and Nkosi dashes from tarp to tarp as he winds through the stalls in the Greenmarket. Umama has sent him on an errand on the way home from school.

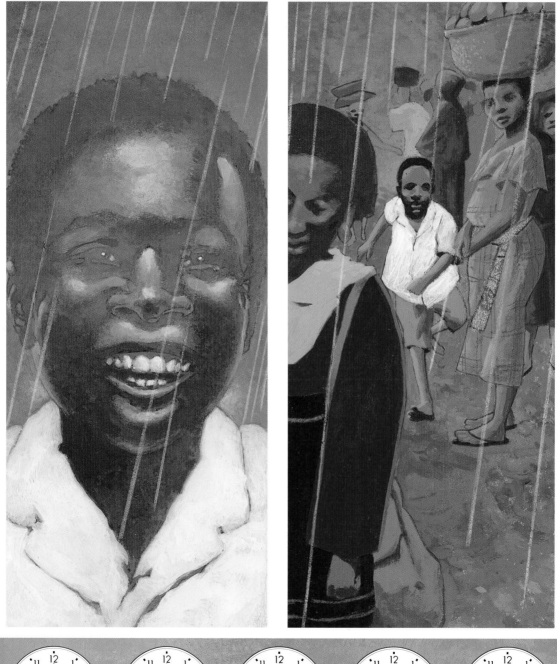

SAN FRANCISCO   MONTRÉAL   SANTIAGO   LONDON   CAPE TOWN

Nkosi stops to run his finger over some used CDs.

"Do you have money today?" the man behind the table asks.

"Today I have many rand," he answers. "But some are to buy washing powder for Umama."

"Choose quickly, my boy," the man says with a wink. "Best not to keep laundry, or mothers, waiting."

LAHORE – 7:00 P.M.

When it's six o'clock in San Francisco, it's seven o'clock in Lahore. Rashida's eyes water and her tongue burns. She reaches for the basket of chapati on the loaded dinner table.

"Too hot for you?" her father teases. Mama's dal is spicier than most cooks' in Pakistan.

"No, it is good," she answers, using the flat bread to ease the fire.

SAN FRANCISCO   MONTRÉAL   SANTIAGO   LONDON   CAPE TOWN

As her father takes a large mouthful of stew, his face reddens and he starts to cough. Rashida passes the cucumber raita to him. The yogurt will cool the burning. Hand over her mouth, she glances at her father and tries very hard not to laugh.

LAHORE

BEIJING – 10:00 P.M.

When it's six o'clock in San Francisco, it's ten o'clock in Beijing. Min-Yue watches his breath sparkle in the frosty air. The ride home from his grandparents' house is short but cold.

Balanced on the back of the bicycle, Min-Yue uses his father's broad back as protection from the wind.

"At least it is not snowing," his mother says, pedaling beside them. The stars shimmer like icicles as they peek around the tops of the buildings.

SAN FRANCISCO   MONTREAL   SANTIAGO   LONDON   CAPE TOWN

LAHORE

BEJING

"Ba', I'm tired," Min-Yue calls.
"Hold on tight," his father answers. "We'll be home soon."
Pressing his head against his father's warm coat, he watches the street rush by under the spinning tires.

SAN FRANCISCO   MONTRÉAL   SANTIAGO   LONDON   CAPE TOWN

LAHORE   BEJING

SYDNEY – 1:00 A.M.

When it's six o'clock in San Francisco, it's one o'clock in Sydney. Alkira should be asleep, but instead she's listening for her father's footsteps on the stairs. Her eyes fly open as she hears the front door creak.

"Daddy, can I have some water?" she calls into the darkness.

"Of course," he whispers from the hallway.

SAN FRANCISCO   MONTRÉAL   SANTIAGO   LONDON   CAPE TOWN

A moment later he tiptoes into the bedroom, a glass of cool water in his hand. Hot and thirsty, she drains it in one gulp. Daddy bends down to kiss her good night. Just back from his shift in the taxi, he smells of car exhaust and gasoline. Alkira loves these smells because they mean he is home from work at last.

"Good night, Daddy," she says softly, half-asleep already. He takes the empty glass and slips quietly out of the room.

LAHORE   BEIJING   SYDNEY

HONOLULU – 4:00 A.M.

When it's six o'clock in San Francisco, it's four o'clock in Honolulu. Keilana rolls over in bed and watches the shadows in the thin line of light peeking under her door. She hears muffled voices and smells strong coffee. Grabbing her blanket, she opens the door and squints into bright light.

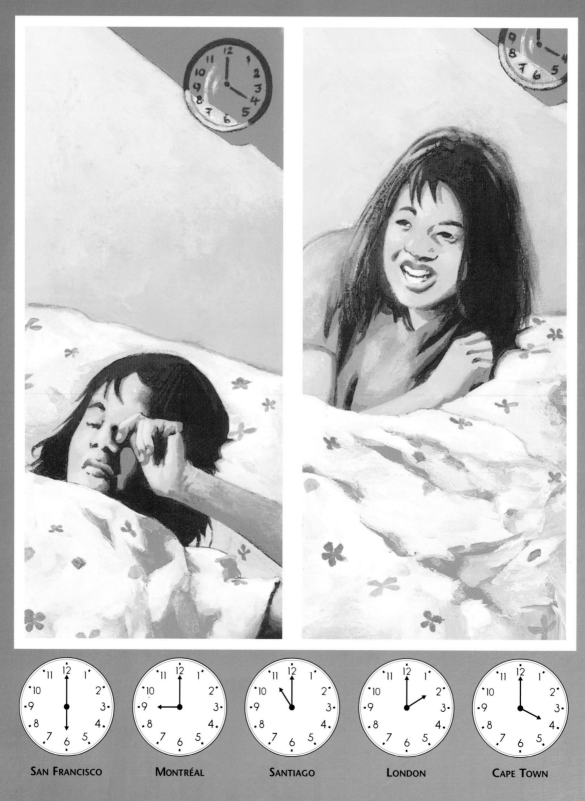

| SAN FRANCISCO | MONTRÉAL | SANTIAGO | LONDON | CAPE TOWN |

"Oh, baby, sorry we woke you," Mommy says, glancing at Daddy.
"Why is your surfboard in the kitchen?" Keilana asks him.
"Waimea Bay has beautiful waves right now," he tells her.
"I want to get some surfing in before work."

LAHORE   BEJING   SYDNEY   HONOLULU

SAN FRANCISCO   MONTRÉAL   SANTIAGO   LONDON   CAPE TOWN

"You can stay up until Daddy leaves. Then it's back to bed," Mommy says, kissing her on the forehead. Keilana climbs onto her lap. She wonders how to convince Mommy to let her stay up for good.

LAHORE   BEJING   SYDNEY   HONOLULU

It's six o'clock in San Francisco. Jared kicks his feet under the table as he wraps his cold fingers around the mug of hot cocoa.

"Peanut butter or bologna?" Mom asks, grabbing his lunchbox from the top of the fridge.

"Bologna, please," he answers.

SAN FRANCISCO   MONTRÉAL   SANTIAGO   LONDON   CAPE TOWN

The ringing telephone pierces the quiet morning.

"Must be Grandma," his mother says, reaching for the phone. "She's the only one who calls this early."

"But it's not that early at Grandma's house," Jared says, blowing the steam off his cocoa. "When it's six o'clock in San Francisco, it's nine o'clock in New York City."

| LAHORE | BEJING | SYDNEY | HONOLULU | NEW YORK |

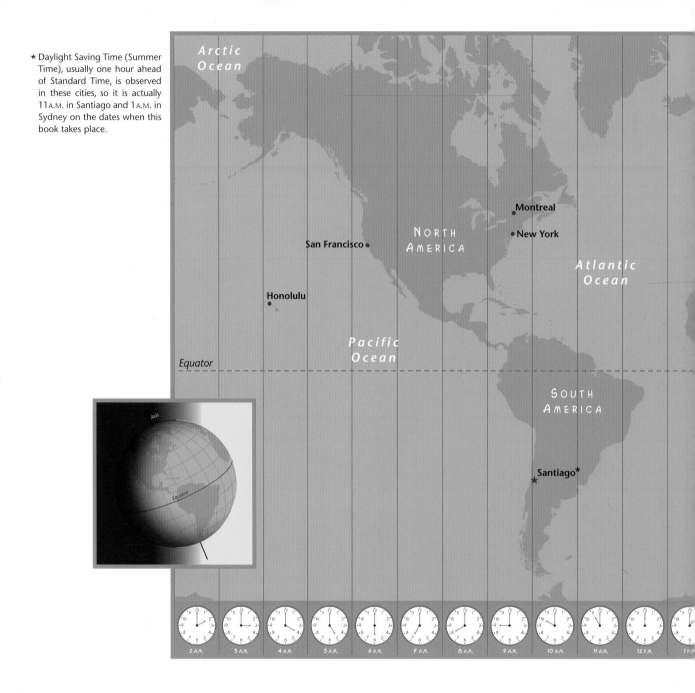

* Daylight Saving Time (Summer Time), usually one hour ahead of Standard Time, is observed in these cities, so it is actually 11 A.M. in Santiago and 1 A.M. in Sydney on the dates when this book takes place.

Arctic Ocean

Montreal

New York

NORTH AMERICA

San Francisco

Atlantic Ocean

Honolulu

Pacific Ocean

Equator

SOUTH AMERICA

Santiago*

Axis

Equator

2 A.M. 3 A.M. 4 A.M. 5 A.M. 6 A.M. 7 A.M. 8 A.M. 9 A.M. 10 A.M. 11 A.M. 12 P.M. 1 P.M.

WHAT TIME IS IT THERE? TIMEKEEPING AND TIME ZONES

TELLING TIME WITH THE SUN

A long time ago, there were no clocks, so people looked at the sun to tell time. When the sun was high overhead, they knew that it was the middle of the day. When the sun dropped down to touch the earth, they knew the day was almost over.

The first clocks were called "sundials," and they used the sun to cast a shadow on the clock face. These early clocks gave only a general idea of the time of day, and they didn't work when it was dark or cloudy. Then, several hundred years ago, mechanical clocks were invented, and timekeeping became much more accurate. But these mechanical clocks were still set according to where the sun was in the sky.

Because the earth is round, when the sun is high in the sky on one side of the earth, it is dark on the other side. As the earth turns, the sun touches different parts of the earth at different times. Even in cities that are only a short distance apart, the sun is at a slightly different place in the sky. So when people set their clocks by the sun, the time was slightly different in each city. Before modern transportation and communication, these differences didn't really matter.

TWENTY-FOUR TIME ZONES

However, once people started traveling by train, these time differences became a problem. Because the clocks in each city were not set to a standard time, passengers didn't know exactly when the trains would arrive. In 1883, railroad companies divided the United States into four standard time

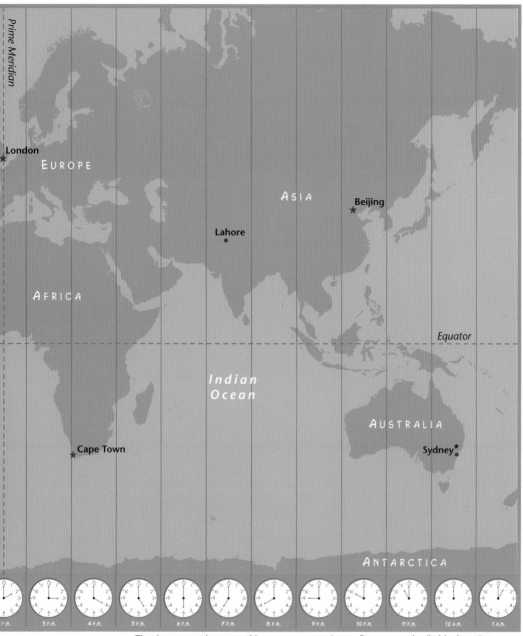

The time zones shown on this map are approximate. For a more detailed look at time zone boundaries throughout the world, you can visit www.hammondmap.com/catalog/maintz.html, search for "world time zones map" on the Internet, or consult an atlas at your local library.

zones. The following year, Greenwich Mean Time was established by an international committee, and standard time zones were set throughout the world.

There are twenty-four hours in a day, so the earth is divided into twenty-four time zones, each one running in a long strip from the North Pole to the South Pole. The time changes by one hour when you move from one time zone to the next.

To find out what time it is in another part of the world, you need to know how many time zones it is from where you are. For example, New York City is three time zones ahead of San Francisco, so when it's six o'clock in San Francisco, it's nine o'clock in New York City. Lahore, Pakistan, is thirteen time zones ahead of San Francisco, so when it's six o'clock in the morning in San Francisco, it's seven o'clock at night in Lahore. (Don't forget to start over at one o'clock when you pass twelve o'clock!)

Seasons Around the World

The seasons are also different in different parts of the world. The earth is tilted sideways on its axis just a little bit. An imaginary line around the middle of the earth called the Equator divides it into the Northern and Southern Hemispheres.

As the earth moves in its orbit around the sun, it is winter in the hemisphere that is tilted away from the sun and summer in the hemisphere that is tilted toward it. As the sun warms different parts of the earth, seasons change. When it is the middle of winter and cold in San Francisco, it is the middle of summer and warm in Sydney, Australia.

For Jaron and Taemon and their cousins around the world
—C.J.O.

To my wonderful wife, Olivia, and our two amazing boys,
Sakai and Matthias, with love
—R.D.B.

Clarion Books
215 Park Avenue South, New York, NY 10003
Text copyright © 2009 by Cynthia Jaynes Omololu
Illustrations copyright © 2009 by Randy DuBurke

The illustrations were executed in pen and ink and acrylic.
The text was set in 13-point Stone Sans.
Map by Kayley LeFaiver

Clarion Books is an imprint of Houghton Mifflin Harcourt Publishing Company

www.clarionbooks.com

Printed in Singapore.

Omololu, Cynthia Jaynes.
When it's six o'clock in San Francisco / by Cynthia Jaynes Omololu ; illustrated by Randy DuBurke.
p. cm.
Summary: When Jared wakes up in San Francisco at six o'clock in the morning, children in other parts
of the world are doing other things, like going to school in Buenos Aires, Argentina, playing soccer in
London, England, and eating dinner in Lahore, Pakistan, because of the difference in time zones
around the globe. Includes factual material about telling time and time zones.
ISBN: 978-0-618-76827-1
[Time—Fiction.] I. DuBurke, Randy, ill. II. Title.
PZ7.O54858 Si 2008
[E]—22   2007012721

TWP 10 9 8 7 6 5 4 3 2 1